Stinky!

By Ann Bryant

Illustrated by Andy Elkerton

Crabtree Publishing Company

www.crabtreebooks.com

Crabtree Publishing Company
www.crabtreebooks.com
1-800-387-7650

616 Welland Ave.
St. Catharines, ON
L2M 5V6

PMB 59051, 350 Fifth Ave.
59th Floor,
New York, NY 10118

Published by Crabtree Publishing Company in 2015

First published in 2013 by Franklin Watts
(A division of Hachette Children's Books)

Text © Ann Bryant 2013
Illustration © Andy Elkerton 2013

Series editor: Melanie Palmer
Series advisor: Catherine Glavina
Series designer: Peter Scoulding
Editors: Jackie Hamley, Kathy Middleton
**Proofreader and
   notes to adults:** Shannon Welbourn
**Production coordinator and
   Prepress technician:** Katherine Berti
Print coordinator: Katherine Berti

Printed in Hong Kong/082014/BK20140613

**Library and Archives Canada
Cataloguing in Publication**

Bryant, Ann, author
     Stinky! / by Ann Bryant ; illustrated by Andy
Elkerton.

(Race ahead with reading)
Issued in print and electronic formats.
ISBN 978-0-7787-1289-3 (bound).--
ISBN 978-0-7787-1334-0 (pbk.)
ISBN 978-1-4271-7780-3 (pdf).--
ISBN 978-1-4271-7768-1 (html)

     I. Elkerton, Andy, illustrator II. Title.

PZ7.B873St 2014   j823'.92   C2014-903689-2
                                          C2014-903690-6

**Library of Congress
Cataloging-in-Publication Data**

Bryant, Ann.
 Stinky! / by Ann Bryant ; illustrated by Andy
Elkerton.
       pages cm. -- (Race ahead with reading)
 "First published in 2013 by Franklin Watts"--
Copyright page.
   ISBN 978-0-7787-1289-3 (reinforced library
binding) -- ISBN 978-0-7787-1334-0 (pbk.) --
ISBN 978-1-4271-7780-3 (electronic pdf) --
ISBN 978-1-4271-7768-1 (electronic html)
 [1. Guinea pigs--Training--Fiction.] I. Elkerton,
Andy, illustrator. II. Title.

PZ7.B8298St 2014
[E]--dc23
                                          2014020441

Chapter One

"Bill Brady is a circus trainer, only with guinea pigs not lions!"

That's what everyone in my class says. But it's not true. I should know. I am Bill Brady.

This is how it started. One day at school, Jimmy Frape was boasting that he had read a book with 100 pages in it.

Then Dan Potter said he was the greatest swimmer ever.

Next Ellen Carr went on and on about galloping on her pony.

Then they all looked at me...like they were waiting.

So, quick as a flash, I made up a story in my head about the guinea pig next door. (It's named Stinky, by the way.) The next thing I know, this came out of my mouth. "I'm training my guinea pig for an animal tricks competition."

Well, you should have seen Ellen Carr's eyebrows. They shot right up to her hairband.

EARTH

Aa Bb Cc

"Bet there's no such thing," said Dan Potter, sounding like a big know-it-all.

I just shrugged and said, "Oh no?"

(That made me feel super cool.)

But only for a moment because Jimmy
Frape suddenly said, "Prove it!"

Then lots of people were crowding around
me saying, "Prove it, Bill! Prove it!"

Chapter Two

I didn't make it up about Stinky. He really can do tricks. Well, one trick anyway. I've seen him do it from my bedroom window.

He jumps over yellow things like buttercups and dandelions.

On the way home from school I figured out a brilliant plan. First I had to borrow Stinky from Mrs. Buss, his owner. So I went around to her house. This was our conversation.

ME: Can Stinky come out to play, please?

MRS. BUSS: (laughing her head off) But he's a guinea pig!

Then she looked at what I was holding and laughed even more.

MRS. BUSS: Blocks! Is that what you two are going to play with?

ME: (still polite) Would you like me to clean out his cage?

MRS. BUSS (sweeter): Super! Thank you, Bill!

I cleaned out Stinky's cage double quick then started his training. First I connected ten yellow blocks together in a line and put them on the grass in front of him. "Okay, jump over these, Stinky!"

He didn't move. So I did a few jumps over the blocks myself, just to show him. It didn't work. He just turned his back.

"That's very rude!" I told him sternly.

"Squeak," he replied.

"You are hopeless!" I said.

"Squeak!" he replied.

Chapter Three

I went next door to train Stinky every day after school. By the fifth day, he could climb up twenty yellow-block steps, walk along a yellow-block bridge, and climb down the other side.

By the tenth day, he managed to wiggle his bottom in and out of fifteen yellow-block posts, then jump over a bridge.

"Fantastic!" cried Mrs. Buss, clapping and clapping.

"Yes," I agreed, feeling happy as a clam.

"I think Mister Stinky is ready for school!"

First I had to ask the teacher, Miss Tate, if I was allowed to bring a guinea pig into class.

"He can do amazing tricks," I informed her in front of the whole class.

"What fun!" cried Miss Tate, clasping her hands together.

I heard Dan snickering, but I didn't mind. In fact, I couldn't wait to see the look on his face when he saw what a great trainer I was.

Chapter Four

"Okay everybody, nice and quiet please," said Miss Tate. We don't want to frighten... er, what's his name?"

"Tricky," I replied, because I didn't want anyone laughing at the name Stinky. I only wanted oohs and aahs and claps.

I set up the yellow-block steps and the bridge and the posts. I felt so excited at that moment, I could have burst.

When everything was ready I took Stinky out of his box and put him down beside the bridge. "Off you go, Stin...I mean, Tricky."

But all he did was squeak
and sit on his bottom.
"Go on!" I said firmly.
But all he did was wriggle.
"Hurry up!" I said loudly.
But all he did was grunt.
"Get going, Stinky!"
I said crossly.

24

And he waddled off leaving a big pile of brown poo right in the middle of the classroom floor.

That made the whole class laugh, including Miss Tate. I went as red as a splotch of ketchup.

Chapter Five

Miss Tate called me up to the front
when it was nearly time to go home.
"You have been wearing that scowl
all afternoon, Bill," she said.
"I know. I'm cross," I replied.

"Maybe Tricky didn't feel like performing
today," she said.
"But no one believes that he really can
do it!" I said grumpily.

Miss Tate frowned. "Can he really do it, Bill?"

"Yes!"

"And are you entering him in an animal tricks competition like you told Dan and the others?" Miss Tate went on.

My face felt hot enough to cook a fried egg on. Miss Tate was going to tell me off now for making things up.

"It's just that I was wondering," she said, "if you could give me the details. You see, my friend has a guinea pig. I'm sure she'd like to enter him, too. He's very talented." "What's his name?" I asked in a little voice.

"Stinky!" she replied.

Uh-oh, I thought.

But then I turned at the sound of gasps.

And this is what I saw. Stinky had come out of his box and was balancing on his hind legs on the top of Dan Potter's yellow soccer ball.

I tell you, I've never heard so many oohs and aahs. It was fantastic.

And as everyone clapped and clapped, a big arc of yellow pee come spraying out of Stinky and onto the floor.

"How did you get him to do that?" asked Jimmy Frape, his eyes all big and round.

Ellen cried, "Because Bill Brady is a circus trainer, only with guinea pigs, not lions!" And I smiled to myself. This time it was true.

Notes for Adults

These entertaining, first chapter books help children build up their reading skills so they can move on to longer books. Fun illustrations and bite-sized chapters encourage young readers to take the driver's seat and *Race Ahead with Reading*.

THE FOLLOWING BEFORE, DURING, AND AFTER READING ACTIVITY SUGGESTIONS SUPPORT LITERACY SKILL DEVELOPMENT AND CAN ENRICH SHARED READING EXPERIENCES:

BEFORE

1. Make reading fun! Choose a time to read when you and the reader are relaxed and have time to share the story together. Don't forget to give praise! Children learn best in a positive environment.
2. Before reading, ask the reader to look at the title and illustration on the cover of the book **Stinky!** Invite them to make predictions about what will happen in the story. They may make use of prior knowledge and make connections to other stories they have heard or read about guinea pigs or other performing animals.

DURING

3. Encourage readers to determine unfamiliar words themselves by using clues from the text and illustrations.
4. During reading, encourage the child to review his or her understanding and see if they want to revise their predictions midway. Encourage the reader to make text-to-text connections, choosing a part of the story that reminds them of another story they have read; and text-to-self connections, choosing a part of the story that relates to their own personal experiences; and text-to-world connections, choosing a part of the story that reminds them of something that happened in the real world.

AFTER

5. Ask the reader who the main characters are in this story. Have the child retell the story in their own words. Ask him or her to think about the predictions they made before reading the story. How were they the same or different?

DISCUSSION QUESTIONS FOR KIDS

6. Throughout this story, Bill Brady is presented with problems. How does he solve the problems he faces?
7. Choose one of the illustrations from the story. How do the details in the picture help you understand a part of the story better? Or, what do they tell you that is not in the text?
8. How did Bill Brady get himself into a bad situation?
9. In the end, Stinky does perform for Bill, and none of his classmates found out that he had lied. Can you think of a time that you stretched the truth? What happened?
10. Have you ever taught a pet to do a trick? Explain. Or, what tricks would you like to teach a pet to do?
11. Create your own story or drawing about a problem or challenge you had and how you solved it.